Cayuga Island Kids

The Mystery of the Barking Branches and the Sunken Ship

Story by
Judy Bradbury

Illustrations by
Gabriella Vagnoli

A City of Light Imprint

Cross Your Fingers
A City of Light imprint

 City of Light Publishing
266 Elmwood Ave. Suite 407
Buffalo, New York 14222

info@CityofLightPublishing.com
www.CityofLightPublishing.com

Written by Judy Bradbury
Illustrated by Gabriella Vagnoli
Book design by Ana Cristina Ochoa

ISBN 978-1-952536-14-4 (softcover)
ISBN 978-1-952536-16-8 (hardcover)
ISBN 978-1-952536-15-1 (eBook)

Printed in Canada
10 9 8 7 6 5 4 3 2 1

Library of Congress Cataloging-in-Publication Data

Names: Bradbury, Judy, author. | Vagnoli, Gabriella, 1979- illustrator.
Title: The mystery of the barking branches and the sunken ship / story by
    Judy Bradbury ; illustrations by Gabriella Vagnoli.
Description: Buffalo, New York : Cross Your Fingers, a City of Light
    imprint, [2021] | Series: Cayuga Island Kids ; book one | Audience: Ages
    8-12. | Audience: Grades 4-6. | Summary: On the first day of summer
    vacation, four mystery-loving friends on a small island are seeking a
    dogwood tree when they unearth a remnant of a famous battleship built in
    the 1600s.
Identifiers: LCCN 2020047274 (print) | LCCN 2020047275 (ebook) | ISBN
    9781952536144 (paperback) | ISBN 9781952536168 (hardcover) | ISBN
    9781952536151 (epub) | ISBN 9781952536151 (kindle edition) | ISBN
    9781952536151 (mobi) | ISBN 9781952536151 (pdf)
Subjects: CYAC: Mystery and detective stories. | Antiquities--Fiction. |
    Griffon (Ship)--Fiction. | Friendship--Fiction. | Islands--Fiction.
Classification: LCC PZ7.B71645 Mym 2021 (print) | LCC PZ7.B71645 (ebook)
    | DDC [E]--dc23
LC record available at https://lccn.loc.gov/2020047274
LC ebook record available at https://lccn.loc.gov/2020047275

*For my dear cousin Lynne Scalia,
who sent me the newspaper article that started it all.*

J.B.

Adventures await!

Judy Bradbury

The Cayuga Island Kids

LACEY

MAC

Other Cayuga Island Characters

MRS. SCHIEBER

MR. ESPOSITO

JULIAN   MAYA   YOKO

MISS LYNNE

DR. SYLVIA SPINA

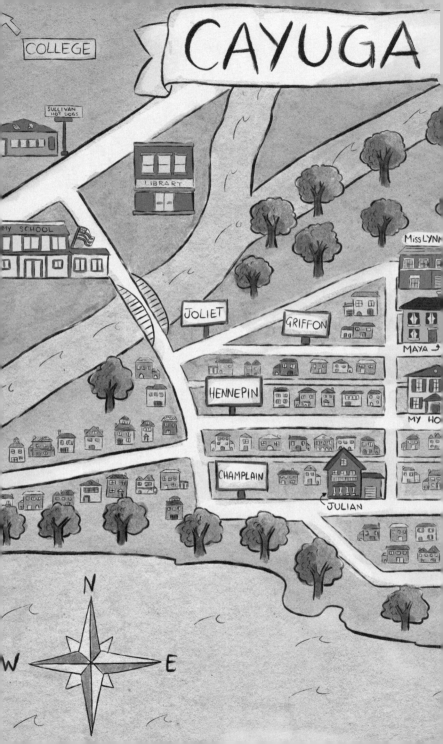

Cayuga Island

Cayuga Island is a tiny island. It is just a few miles upstream from the mighty Niagara Falls, one of the Seven Wonders of the World. A narrow bridge leads on and off the island. It crosses where the churning Niagara River narrows to a gurgling creek.

Four streets run the length of the island. Three of them are named for explorers of the Niagara Frontier: Joliet, Hennepin, and Champlain. The fourth street is named after a ship, the Griffon. Gravel alleys wind behind the houses. There are seven.

But there are no schools or stores, no stoplights or movie theaters or much of anything else on the island—except fun, adventure, and perhaps a bit of mystery, if you look for it.

It's summer now, and that's what the Cayuga Island Kids plan to do. Are you ready to join their adventure?

Contents

CHAPTER ONE

The Cayuga Island Kids

Under the covers, something was tickling Lacey.

She wiggled her toes. She waggled her foot. It was the first day of summer vacation, and Lacey wasn't ready to open her eyes.

Tickle. Tickle.

Lacey jiggled and joggled her foot. She scratched her big toe with her other big toe.

The tickle scurried up her leg to her shin. It teased her knee.

Lacey flung back the covers. It was time to solve the first mystery of summer vacation.

Pesky lifted his furry head. His shaggy tail spun in circles.

"Yip!" yapped Pesky.

Lacey patted her pup. "Mystery solved!"

At Mac's house something was tickling his ear.

Mac shook his head. His hands were busy dumping Pop-Pops from the hero-sized cereal box into his frontiersman bowl. Ever since he found out about the American Old West, no other bowl would do. Besides, it was good and deep, and Mac was as hungry as a bear in spring.

Tickle. Tickle.

Mac's hands were busy pouring milk over the cereal, so he shook his head a little harder.

Milk splished and splashed onto the table.

Mac swiped it with his sleeve. Then he reached up to itch the tickle.

The furry tail on his coonskin cap swished. It wasn't really raccoon fur—Mac wouldn't like that. But it was his dad's hat when he was a boy, and Mac really liked that.

Soon Mac wasn't as hungry as a bear anymore. He picked up his powder horn and slung it over his shoulder. He was ready for his first adventure of summer!

At Julian's house, the *Junior Scientist's Word-of-the-Day* was tickling his brain.

Dogwood. What a funny name for a tree!

Julian wondered. What does a dogwood look like? How did the tree get its name? Do the branches wag like a dog's tail?

Julian tapped on his tablet. He swiped and read. *When the wind blows, the branches of the dogwood sound like a dog barking.*

Julian giggled. Bark barking!

Julian read on. *Long ago dogwood stems were used to make toothbrushes, tennis rackets, and arrows.*

Arrows! Julian giggled again. Wait until Mac hears that!

Julian wondered. Are there dogwood trees on Cayuga Island?

Well, it was summer now, and that meant there was plenty of time to find out.

A breeze tickled Maya's nose. A bee buzzed against the screen on her bedroom window.

Maya stretched and rose. She twirled to the closet and put on her most favorite purple ballet shoes.

The elastic hugged her foot. Satin ribbons brushed her ankles as she wound them around her legs.

Maya danced down the hall, through the kitchen, and out the door.

She sat on the purple seat of her most favorite swing set her dad had built for her.

Maya leaned back and began to fly.

A curl tickled her face as she climbed higher.

Maya rose above her most favorite sandbox with its purple-striped awning. She looked across the yard.

Purple tee shirts, purple shorts, and purple leotards waved from the clothesline.

Sparky the cat lay beside the bushes. Her purple collar sparkled in the sun.

Maya spotted a chickadee in the broad elm tree. It chirped a welcome as another chickadee flew near.

Maya folded her legs and pulled.

Higher and higher she went.

As she swung forward, Maya spied something. It was furry with a stripy tail, and it was bobbing along the sidewalk on the other side of the fence.

What was that?

Before Maya could puzzle it out, she was swinging backwards.

When she arced up again, the furry thing with the stripy tail was gone.

Mysterious, she thought. And that made her think of Lacey.

"Maya!" a voice called out. "Want to go to the park?"

The chickadees flew off. Sparky scampered across the yard.

Maya turned to find a furry cap with a stripy tail sitting on top of Mac's head.

Mystery solved!

The bell buzzed and Yoko answered the door.

Maya twirled. "Come with us to the park."

"It's summer!" Mac's cap bobbed. "Adventures await!"

Yoko's eyes sparkled. What could be better than two friends at your door?

"It's sunny and bright,

Not a cloud in sight.

I'm ready to play

the summer away."

The rhyme tickled Yoko's brain. Making rhymes always did that.

Maybe it was because even her name rhymed. Yoko liked to say it was the shortest poem ever.

She reached for her sunglasses and clicked the door shut.

What could be better than two friends at your door?

Yoko grinned. Two friends at your door on a summer day, that's what.

Yoko loved to rhyme. She loved summer. And she loved being with her friends.

CHAPTER TWO

Mystery or Hunt?

I n the park Julian was looking up at a tree.

"What's up?" Mac asked.

Yoko giggled.

Maya balanced on her toes. She circled her arms around her head and looked up.

"Does this tree look like this one?" Julian pointed from the tree in front of them to the tree in the photo on his tablet.

Yoko rhymed an answer.

"These trees are not alike.

These leaves curve, those spike."

"This is a dogwood." Julian tapped the tablet. "Its branches make a barking sound when they rub together."

"Really?" Maya looked down at the tablet and lost her balance.

Julian rubbed one of the tree's branches against another. No barking.

He read more from the tablet. "Its branches have been used to make toothbrushes, tennis rackets, and arrows."

"Arrows!" Suddenly, Mac was very interested.

Maya studied the photos. "Its blossoms are pretty." She wondered if they smelled good.

With a yip and a yap, Pesky joined the group. Lacey was close behind.

"Show Lacey the photo of the tree,
She can help solve this mystery."

Yoko loved that *tree* and *mystery* rhymed.

Lacey's eyes widened. "Mystery?"

"We want to find a dogwood tree," explained Julian.

"So we can make arrows for our adventures!" The tail on Mac's cap swished.

"And braid the blossoms into a tiara," added Maya.

"And listen to it bark," said Julian.

Lacey wasn't sure what Julian meant by that. But she was stuck on something else. "This seems more like a hunt than a mystery," she said.

"A hunt is an adventure!" Mac was really excited now.

"The mystery is if there are any dogwood trees on Cayuga Island. The adventure is hunting for one." Julian wanted to keep both Lacey and Mac interested.

"Yip," said Pesky. He ran in circles chasing his tail.

Lacey laughed. "I guess Pesky wants to hunt for a *dog*wood tree, too."

"Adventure awaits!" cried Mac. He felt like an explorer on the frontier.

CHAPTER THREE

Clues

"Wait," said Lacey. She pulled a notebook from her back pocket and a pencil from behind her ear. "We need clues."

Lacey kept notes on the clues she found and the mysteries she hoped to solve in a notebook. She flipped to a blank page. She wrote Dogwood Trees at the top. "Ready," she said.

"The dogwood has pretty flowers." Maya pointed to the picture on the tablet.

Julian read the caption. "The dogwood has white, pink, or red leaves called bracts with yellow flowers in the center."

Lacey took notes.

Julian pointed to the screen on his tablet. "It also says, 'Dogwoods bloom in the spring.'" He frowned. "It's summer now, so the blooms will be gone."

Lacey crossed out the clue she had just written down.

Maya was disappointed. "Then what will we make tiaras from?"

Yoko had an idea.

"We'll gather and weave the leaves instead,
Then glue on a jewel or two.
Add sparkle and shine to the top of your head
And gems to the toes of each shoe!"

Maya twirled in one direction and then the other. She liked sparkle as much as she liked flowers.

Lacey frowned at her notes. "We need a few more clues to help us find a dogwood tree."

Julian read on.

Yoko listened for words she could rhyme.

Maya practiced holding her head high. That was important so her tiara—once she had one—wouldn't slip off.

Pesky wagged his tail.

Lacey took notes.

Mac reached into his powder horn and pulled out a stash of candies. All this reading and searching for clues was making him hungry.

Dogwood Trees

- ~~lots of white, pink, or red leaves (called bracts) with yellow flowers in the center in spring~~
- light green leaves in summer
- deep red leaves in fall
- in winter bark looks like alligator skin
- grows 20-30 feet tall
- likes some sun, but not too much
- branches are thin and hard
- when branches rub together, it sounds like a dog barking

Soon Lacey had a list in her notebook. She would cross out anything the kids decided weren't good clues. The first fact was already crossed out.

"Don't forget that the branches were used to make arrows," Mac reminded his friends.

But Lacey didn't write that down. "Interesting fact, but not a clue," she said.

Julian read on. "In the 1600s, Native Americans knew winter was over and it was time to plant corn when dogwoods bloomed." He scrolled down the page. "They thought dogwoods were lucky." He paused. "The bark and roots from the dogwood tree were used for medicines and dyes. The sap is poisonous."

"We should remember that last fact," said Mac.

It wasn't a clue, but Mac was right. It was important to remember. Lacey added it to the list.

Finally, they were done. Lacey's notes looked like this:

Dogwood Trees

- ~~lots of white, pink, or red leaves (called bracts) with yellow flowers in the center in spring~~
- light green leaves in summer
- ~~deep red leaves in fall~~
- ~~bark looks like alligator skin in winter~~
- grows 20–30 feet tall
- likes some sun, but not too much
- branches are thin and hard
- when branches rub together, it sounds like a dog barking
- the sap is poisonous

Lacey put the notebook in her back pocket. "Our suspects are trees," she announced. "We are detectives!"

"Time to investigate!" Mac rubbed his hands together.

"Where do we start?" Maya looked around the park. "There are trees all over Cayuga Island." She wondered if she would have a tiara by tomorrow.

"You are right," agreed Julian.

"We could ask an expert," Lacey said.

"Mrs. Schieber!" Mac shouted.

Yoko nodded. Mrs. Schieber knew something about everything. She was the school librarian, after all.

Maya pointed her toes and leapt her way out of the park. Mrs. Schieber was her favorite adult at their school.

Pesky tugged on his leash as if he wanted to leap after Maya. Lacey tucked the pencil behind her ear and followed her friends.

Chapter Four

Expert

Mrs. Schieber lived on Hennepin Avenue, a few blocks down from Mac. The street was named after an explorer. Mrs. Schieber liked that because she was curious about history. She had read many books about Father Hennepin and all the explorers of the Niagara Frontier.

Besides history and reading, Mrs. Schieber liked gardening. And now that it was summer, the kids knew they would find Mrs. Schieber in her yard beneath a large straw hat.

She was kneeling, pulling weeds. "Hello, my friends!" She smiled widely. "Are you enjoying the first day of summer vacation?"

"Adventures await!" said Mac.

"Sounds exciting," said Mrs. Schieber. She snipped a cluster of dandelions and turned to Yoko. "I pluck the weeds so they don't spread their…"

"Seeds!" Yoko finished the sentence.

Mrs. Schieber nodded. "But it's also a pleasure to turn trash into…"

"Treasure!" Yoko felt lucky to have Mrs. Schieber as a neighbor as well as the librarian at Cayuga Drive School.

Mrs. Schieber laughed and handed the yellow flowers to Maya. Mrs. Schieber knew Yoko liked to rhyme, and she knew Maya liked flowers. "Just because we call these weeds doesn't mean they're not pretty," she said.

Maya agreed. "I make necklaces from dandelions. I wonder, would they make a good tiara?"

"Anyway," said Julian, hoping to keep his friends on track, "we need the help of an expert."

"That's why we thought of you," said Maya, rubbing her chin against the dandelions.

"We have a mystery to solve," Lacey explained.

Pesky wagged his tail and panted. He had just run two blocks from the park to Mrs. Schieber's garden, after all.

Mrs. Schieber filled a pail with cold water. She put it down in front of Pesky.

"Tell me about this mystery," she said.

"It's a mystery and a hunt and an adventure," said Mac.

"I see," said Mrs. Schieber.

"We are hunting for a dogwood tree," said Julian.

"The mystery is whether there is a dogwood tree on Cayuga Island," Lacey explained.

"I did some research," said Julian.

Mac nodded. The tail on his cap bobbed. "Julian found a ton of facts about dogwoods."

"All mysteries need facts to help get them solved," said Mrs. Schieber.

"I remembered to check more than one source," said Julian, "just like you taught us."

Mrs. Schieber gave Julian a thumbs-up.

"Now we need to detect and inspect a suspect or two," Yoko said. So far, summer was turning out to be a ton of rhyming fun.

"Hunting for suspects can be exciting," Mrs. Schieber said, "especially when you are looking for something that can hide in plain sight."

"Hide in plain sight?" Maya repeated.

Lacey liked the sound of that. Very mysterious. She reached for her notebook.

"When you are hunting for suspects," Mrs. Schieber explained, "you must pay attention to everything. Be observant. Notice every detail. You never know where you will find a clue."

Mrs. Schieber sat in the dirt beside a row of tomato plants. "For instance, did you notice that butterfly?" Mrs. Schieber pointed to a clump of marigolds. A butterfly fluttered its wings and soon flew to another part of the garden. "Or this ladybug?" She fingered a leaf on the tomato plant next to her.

"They would be good suspects if we were looking for garden helpers," Julian joked.

Mrs. Schieber laughed. "That's correct, Julian. Butterflies spread pollen with their wings. A ladybug can eat up to 50 aphids a day. Both garden helpers keep my plants healthy."

Mac leaned in to get a better look at the ladybug. "It makes sense to look for a garden helper in a garden. I wish we knew where to look for a dogwood."

"Start with what you know," said Mrs. Schieber. "And think about what you need to find out."

CHAPTER FIVE

Details

The friends gathered around Lacey's list of clues.

"We know dogwood leaves are light green in summer," said Yoko.

"We don't know the shape of the leaves," said Julian.

"Or their size," said Mac.

Julian typed on his tablet. *What is the size and shape of the dogwood tree leaf?*

A photo and answer popped up in seconds. The kids leaned in. Julian read. "The dogwood tree leaf is 3 to 5 inches long. It is oval in shape with a wavy edge, green above and somewhat paler below."

Lacey wrote the information in her note-book right after the fact that dogwoods grow 20-30 feet tall.

"How tall is 20-30 feet?" Maya wondered.

"I'm four feet tall," said Mac. "I had to stand by a ruler before I was allowed to ride the roller coaster at Fantastic Island."

The kids looked at each other. They measured themselves against Mac. Yoko was a little taller. Lacey was a little shorter. But they were all just about the same height.

"I'm taller if I stand on my tiptoes," said Maya. "I'm even taller if I hold my head high." She showed her friends. They all stood on their tiptoes. They held their heads high. Still, Yoko was a little taller and Lacey was a little shorter than the others.

The kids looked around Mrs. Schieber's yard. There were lots of bushes. Some were shorter than the kids. Some were taller. A bush along the fence was the tallest.

"This bush is more than four feet tall," said Mac.

"I'm six feet tall," said Mrs. Schieber. She stood next to the bush. It was a little shorter than she was. Nothing in the garden was taller than Mrs. Schieber.

Julian thought out loud. "Mrs. Schieber is six feet tall. Five Mrs. Schiebers stacked one on top of the other would be thirty feet—or as tall as a dogwood tree grows."

Mac giggled. "There's only one Mrs. Schieber."

"If we stacked ourselves one on top of the other, how tall would that be?" Maya asked.

"We're all about four feet tall," said Yoko. "So that would be twenty feet!" Yoko was as good at math as she was at rhyming.

"Let's get a visual," suggested Mrs. Schieber.

She told Mac to lie down in the grass. Mrs. Schieber placed a garden trowel beneath his feet.

Lacey lay down next, with her feet just above Mac's cap. Then came Yoko.

"Don't point your toes, no ballet pose," she reminded Maya, who was next.

Julian followed. Mrs. Schieber placed a twig above his head.

Pesky raced for the twig, but Mrs. Schieber was quicker. She placed her foot firmly on top of it.

"Everyone up!" Mrs. Schieber clapped her hands.

The kids looked from the garden trowel to the twig.

"Twenty feet is tall," observed Julian.

Pesky yipped and ran around the twig under Mrs. Schieber's foot.

"How long is this?" Lacey asked, pointing to the hose.

"Why, I believe it's thirty feet!" Mrs. Schieber exclaimed.

The kids stretched the hose out next to where they had lain. A full-grown dogwood could be 20-30 feet tall, and now they knew what that looked like.

All of this research was making Mac hungry. He plucked a tiny tomato from one of Mrs. Schieber's patio plants. It was warm and as sweet as candy.

CHAPTER SIX

The Hunt Begins

"Let's begin our search in the park," suggested Lacey.

The park was narrow and ran alongside a shallow creek off the Niagara River. There were flowers and bushes and grass. And there were plenty of trees.

"Good idea," said Julian. "We can each search a section."

"Buddy up and stay within sight of one another," Mrs. Schieber reminded the kids.

Mac picked up his powder horn and slung it over his shoulder. "Ready," he said.

"Not quite," said Mrs. Schieber. She plucked a handful of the bite-sized tomatoes from the plants on the patio. She dropped them into Mac's powder horn. "Sustenance for the hunt." She winked at Mac.

Mac didn't know the word *sustenance*, but he could figure out what it meant. He wouldn't go hungry as he hunted for a dogwood tree in the park.

Maya carefully tucked the dandelions into the toes of her most favorite purple ballet shoes. They weren't gems, but they sure were pretty. She hoped the flowers would last until they found a dogwood tree.

Julian took one last look at the length of hose. He studied the space between the garden trowel and the twig. He checked the photo of the dogwood tree leaf on his tablet. Finally, he was ready.

Yoko pushed up her sunglasses and fist-bumped Mrs. Schieber.

"We'd like to stay, but we can't delay.

We have a mystery to solve today."

Mrs. Schieber waved goodbye as the friends headed back to the park.

Trees were all around, just as they had been before they visited Mrs. Schieber. But now the Cayuga Island Kids had a plan.

They had gathered facts.

They knew important details.

They would buddy up.

They would look for clues hiding in plain sight.

The hunt was on!

They would find a dogwood in no time.

Or so they thought.

CHAPTER SEVEN

Buddies

Maya and Yoko linked arms. They would be buddies. Maya stopped at a patch of wildflowers as soon as they entered the park. Yoko waited. She was Maya's buddy, after all. And buddies stick together.

Pesky stopped, too. He liked sniffing things, and the park was the perfect place for that. When Lacey tried to move him along, he dug in his heels.

"He can buddy up with us," Yoko said, and Lacey handed her the leash.

Lacey followed Julian. He was the perfect buddy. Julian had gathered the facts. Lacey had written them down. They could check facts in Lacey's notebook or on Julian's tablet. They would solve this mystery.

Mac followed Julian, too. He was the perfect buddy. Julian was Mac's best friend, after all. Besides that, Julian was very good at research. He could investigate how to make arrows—once they found a dogwood tree.

Three people could buddy up.

Julian spotted a tree that seemed to be the right height. He pointed. "Maybe that one?"

Lacey looked up. Mac looked up, too.

Julian and Lacey studied the leaves. Were they the right shape?

Mac studied the branches. "These are too thick to be dogwoods. They wouldn't make good arrows," he said.

Julian and Lacey looked at the branches.

"You're right," said Lacey.

Julian agreed.

They kept walking. Julian followed Mac. Lacey followed Mac, too. They made a good team of three.

Back at the flowers, Maya bent down to sniff a purple bloom. Would it be okay to pick this most favorite flower to put behind her ear?

Yoko didn't think so.

"If every person picked a bloom
public gardens would be doomed.
Enjoy them with your nose and eyes
leave picking and plucking to the gardening guys."

And gardening girls, thought Maya. But she knew why Yoko didn't say that. *Guys* rhymes with *eyes*. *Girls* doesn't.

Maya noticed Pesky pawing at something. She leaned over and looked closer.

On the edge of the patch of wildflowers was a round, hard bump.

What was that?

It was covered in dirt, but it didn't look like part of a plant.

Was it a rock?

Was it a nest?

Or was something buried there?

Chapter Eight

A Bump in the Park

Maya leaned in even closer. Pesky wagged. Maya helped Pesky brush away more of the dirt.

Maya pulled on Yoko's arm. "This is not a rock or part of a plant. Something is buried here."

Together the girls scraped at the dirt. Pesky, too. They made a good team of three.

Soon they could see more of the hard, round bump. It looked like it was about the size of a softball. But it felt cold, like metal.

Yoko pushed up her sunglasses.

"We need something to dig out this ball,

It's stuck in there and it isn't small."

She snapped her fingers.

"I know what we can do!

Borrow a trowel from you-know-who!"

"Great idea," Maya said. "Pesky and I will stay here to mark the spot."

Yoko ran all the way to Mrs. Schieber's house.

Meanwhile, Mac, Julian, and Lacey walked slowly through the park. They looked left and right. They looked up. They eyed each tree. Would they find a dogwood hiding in plain sight?

Some trees were too tall. Other trees had blossoms or pine cones. Many trees were the wrong shape. None of the leaves matched the photos on Julian's tablet.

The three friends looked and looked. When they reached the far end of the park, Lacey pulled out her notebook. She studied the list of facts. She wanted to be sure they hadn't missed a clue.

Julian looked over her shoulder.

Mac sighed. He reached into his powder horn and pulled out a tiny tomato. It was round and plump and warm. He popped it into his mouth and tasted its goodness. He reached into his horn for another.

Lacey held out her hand. Mac gave her the tomato. He tossed another one to Julian.

The kids enjoyed the tomatoes and then turned around. They had walked to the end of the park. It was time to head back.

Lacey led the way. Julian followed. He was still studying the trees. Maybe he would see something he missed. Then came Mac. He was fishing in his powder horn, hoping for another tomato.

CHAPTER NINE

Buried Treasure

Up ahead the girls were waving. Maya was jumping up and down. Or was she dancing?

Pesky yipped. He seemed to be dancing, too. Or was he just jumping up and down?

"Is that a garden shovel in Yoko's hand?" Lacey wondered out loud. She hurried ahead.

Julian followed. Mac was close behind.

Yoko and Maya showed their friends what they had uncovered.

"We think it's a metal ball," said Maya.

First Julian, then Mac, then Lacey took a turn digging with the small garden shovel. They were careful. They didn't want to damage the ball. Slowly they wiped away more and more of the dirt.

Julian felt around the ball. "It's solid, and it seems heavy," he said.

"I wonder where it came from," said Maya.

"I wonder how long it's been here," added Yoko.

"It looks old," said Mac.

Lacey's eyes sparkled. "We *uncovered* another mystery..." She eyed her friends to see if they got the joke she had made. "I'll add it to our first mystery." She flipped to a new page in her notebook. "This is the best day ever!"

"A mystery ball..." Maya giggled. "That sounds like a fairy tale."

Mac had a different thought. "Could it be part of a wagon wheel from the frontier days?"

"Or a meteorite?" wondered Yoko.

Julian's forehead wrinkled. That usually meant he was thinking. "This ball is heavy, it's metal, and it looks old. Wait!" Julian snapped his fingers.

"Julian is getting another idea," said Mac.

Julian clicked on his tablet. He swiped and tapped.

A photo popped up and Julian zoomed in.

"This could be a cannonball!" Julian cried.

Maya's eyes grew wide.

Yoko gasped.

Meanwhile, Pesky raced in circles around the ball.

"A cannonball!" Mac looked from Maya to Yoko to Pesky. "You make a terrific team!"

Yoko grinned. In her head, she was already thinking of words that rhyme with cannonball. *Outlet mall, concert hall, ten feet tall...*

CHAPTER TEN

Digging and Digging

J ulian was excited. "Let's get this out of the ground."

The kids worked together to try to free the metal ball.

Yoko began digging first. Maya and Julian knelt beside her and pushed aside the dirt. Lacey dug next. Then Mac. Pesky wagged and yipped at the growing mound.

The kids pushed and pulled the ball. They huffed and puffed in the hot sun. The ball was solid and heavy. It did not move much.

Mac pushed back his coonskin cap.

Yoko wiped her brow.

Maya noticed the flowers on her shoes were wilting.

Suddenly, a shadow moved across the kids. They looked up to find Mr. Esposito peering down at them.

Mr. Esposito was Maya's next-door neighbor. He was also a park volunteer. He kept the park tidy and the flowers blooming.

"What's going on here?" he asked. "Digging in public gardens is not thoughtful of others. And it is not allowed." Mr. Esposito eyed Pesky, but the dog was just sniffing a pile of fresh dirt. It was the kids who had a trowel, and they were dusty from digging.

Mac adjusted his cap. "We're trying to get a cannonball out of the flower bed."

"Mac, you sure do have a powerful imagination. And you're always on the lookout for adventure. But, a cannonball…?" Mr. Esposito cocked his head.

"Well," Julian explained, "we think it *might* be a cannonball." Julian liked to stick to the facts.

Mr. Esposito crouched down.

He took a good look at the metal ball.

He adjusted his glasses.

He scratched away more of the dirt.

"Well, I'll be..." Mr. Esposito sputtered. He was so surprised, he fell onto his behind. His hat fell off and landed in the pile of dirt. Lacey grabbed it just before Pesky got to it.

She brushed it off and handed it to Mr. Esposito.

"We were looking for a dogwood tree, but we found this," said Maya.

Mr. Esposito pointed at the ball. "This is definitely not a dogwood tree."

"We are going to make arrows from dogwood branches," said Mac.

"And tiaras from the leaves," added Maya.

"Once we find a dogwood tree," said Mac.

"Anyway, do you think this could be a cannonball?" asked Julian. He liked to stick to the topic.

Mr. Esposito stood and brushed off the seat of his pants. "Let's see if we can free this ball and have a better look. I'll get a proper tool for the job."

He turned and headed for his garden cart. Mac followed. The garden cart used to be a golf cart, but Mr. Esposito liked gardening more than he liked golf. So he carried garden tools where the golf clubs used to be. Mac thought all the shovels and especially those big scissors were way more interesting than golf clubs.

Mr. Esposito chose a narrow shovel and a small spade. He pulled out his leather work gloves and handed them to Mac to carry. Then he tucked away the clippers. "Trimming the park bushes will have to wait for another day," he said. "We have a cannonball to tend to."

CHAPTER ELEVEN

Investigation

Mr. Esposito wiped his brow with the sleeve of his shirt. He picked up the ball. He held it in both hands and turned it carefully. Even though it was heavy, he treated it as if it were as fragile as a robin's egg.

He passed it to Julian.

"Wow!" Julian whistled. "That's hefty."

Mac held it next. He figured that hefty must mean heavy. He tried to whistle, too, but it came out *whoo–whoo*.

Mr. Esposito took a rag from his back pocket and gently dusted the ball. Bits of metal fell into the dirt.

The kids looked closely at the ball, but there were no markings on it.

Lacey studied the flakes of metal in the dirt. She picked up one of the larger pieces to give it a closer look. She rummaged in her pockets for a tissue and wrapped the flake inside. Carefully, she tucked the folded tissue away. Then she took out her notebook. "Time to investigate," she said.

Julian opened his tablet. "We can start by searching for photos of cannonballs and see if we find one that looks like this," he suggested.

Yoko pushed up her sunglasses.

Meanwhile, Maya sat cross-legged on the ground. She patted Pesky. She wondered if he would like a dandelion dog collar. Plenty of the weeds were flowering. She spotted trailing vines with teeny purple flowers. She especially liked those. She was pretty sure plucking weeds from the park would be allowed. Mr. Esposito might even decide she would make an excellent park volunteer.

Maya was about to ask Mr. Esposito if she could pick the weeds when she noticed her backyard neighbor walking toward them.

Miss Lynne waved. A colorful quilted bag hung from her shoulder. Papers and books poked out of the top. A badge on a ribbon hung from the side. Miss Lynne taught at the college across town, and even though it was summer vacation for the Cayuga Island Kids, Miss Lynne had classes to teach.

"Hello, my friends!" Miss Lynne bent to pet Pesky and noticed the cannonball. "What is that?" she asked.

Mr. Esposito rocked back and forth on his heels. "The kids found it right here," he pointed to the flower bed.

Julian answered Miss Lynne's question. "We think maybe it's a cannonball."

"A cannonball!" she exclaimed.

"Maybe," Julian repeated.

"We're investigating." Lacey pointed to Julian's tablet.

"We want to figure out if this really could be a cannonball," Maya said.

"And how it ended up here," added Yoko.

"There's plenty of history attached to this island," said Miss Lynne. "Three of the streets are named after explorers of the Niagara Frontier. Griffon Avenue was named after their ship."

"That's my street!" Maya exclaimed.

"We were hunting for a dogwood tree to

make arrows. Then we found this," said Mac. "Arrows! Cannonballs! Explorers! *The Niagara Frontier!* I didn't even know we were part of a frontier! This is turning out to be a terrific summer so far."

Suddenly, Julian held out his tablet. "This cannonball looks like a match." His brow crumpled. "But how can we be sure?"

Miss Lynne drummed her chin with her fingers. "Researching on the internet is helpful," she said, "but your public library can be the best place to gather information on local history. Old books and papers stored in special collections are called archives."

Lacey turned the page in her notebook and wrote ARCHIVES in big letters.

Miss Lynne tilted her head as if she were thinking. "College libraries often hold even more items in their archives. You might find answers there. But you have to be a member of a college to use their library." Miss Lynne smiled as she looked from kid to kid.

Maya's eyes grew wide. "Can someone visit a college library with a member?" she asked.

Miss Lynne threw back her head and laughed. "Yes, some *one*—or two or three or more—can visit a college library as guests of a member—and that member would be me!"

Julian whooped.

Mac whooped, too.

Maya reached up to grab her neighbor's hand and twirled into a hug for Miss Lynne.

Yoko was thinking of words that rhyme with archives. *Bee hives, deep-sea dives, fresh chives, high-fives.* That's a good one, she thought.

"High fives for the archives!" she cheered, slapping Lacey's hand.

"Keep me posted," said Mr. Esposito. He hopped into the golf cart.

"Wait!" said Lacey. "Who is going to be in charge of keeping the cannonball?"

"The maybe-cannonball," Julian said.

"Oh, my!" Mr. Esposito hit his forehead and his cap fell off again. "I hadn't thought of that."

"We found it in the park, and the park is public property," said Julian. "It doesn't belong to us."

Stink bug! Mac sighed. He had hoped they could keep the cannonball in his tree house — even if it was only a maybe-cannonball.

"I'll lock it up in the garden shed and contact the city parks department," Mr. Esposito offered.

Julian took a few pictures of the maybe-cannonball with his tablet before Mr. Esposito drove off.

Miss Lynne turned to the kids. "Just thinking about research makes me hungry. How about lunch at Sullivan's Hot Dog Stand before we hit the stacks? My treat."

"Yes!" Mac answered for them all. He wasn't sure what it meant to hit the stacks, but he was sure that Sullivan's had the best hot dogs around.

CHAPTER TWELVE

Primary Sources

The kids found the local history room across from the elevator on the third floor of the college library.

"Shhh," Mac whispered as they entered the room. None of his friends had spoken, but libraries are quiet spaces. Mac wanted to be sure they didn't bother anyone. He looked around. No one was in the local history room except his friends and Miss Lynne.

Lacey walked toward a long glass case in the center of the room. She peered inside. Thin crinkled papers rested beside fancy pens like the kind Sherlock Holmes might have used. There were yellowed newspapers and black and white photos.

The kids spread out around the room. Everywhere they looked, they found a piece of local history.

Some cases held old brass tools. Others held books with gold bindings and frayed satin markers. Wooden plaques told how old the item was and why it was important.

Yoko studied a framed brown and white map with fancy printing that hung on the wall.

"Everything here looks really old," whispered Mac.

"These documents and items are called artifacts," Miss Lynne explained. "They offer an important view into our history."

Lacey tilted her head. "Is an artifact sort of like evidence in a mystery?"

Miss Lynne nodded. "An artifact is something from a particular time in history." She moved aside so Maya could get a better look inside the display case in front of them. "Artifacts are priceless because they are primary sources."

Maya was curious. "What's a primary source?"

"Primary sources offer firsthand information." Miss Lynne pointed to a worn leather diary with initials on the front. "Primary sources can also be accounts from people."

"Like an eye witness!" exclaimed Lacey. "Someone who was there."

"So a primary source would be someone who watches a ballet instead of reading about it in the newspaper or on a blog, or hearing about it on TV or the radio?" said Maya.

Julian nodded. "A primary source also could be someone who performs in the ballet."

Miss Lynne held up a finger. "Keep in mind, though, primary source information can be inaccurate or biased."

"Biased?" repeated Yoko.

"If you and I go to the ballet and we both watch the performance, but you love ballet and I don't, we may have different views of the performance," explained Miss Lynne.

"You might be wishing you were fishing instead," said Mac.

Maya rolled her eyes, but Yoko laughed. Mac had made a rhyme without even realizing it.

Maya turned toward a case holding a model ship. "The Griffon!" she exclaimed, pointing to the plaque.

The kids gathered around. The model ship was made from thin, polished pieces of wood. It was long and narrow. The sides of the ship were curvy. Four masts flew above. A bird-like creature perched on the bow, or the front of the ship. A horse with wings seemed to guard the back of the ship. The plaque said the Griffon was built in 1679. It might have looked like this.

Julian pulled his tablet out of his backpack. "May I take some pictures?" he asked Miss Lynne.

She pointed to a sign on the wall. "As long as you don't use the flash," she said.

Yoko knew why the sign was there.

"A flash is a splash of really bright light
It may not cause damage,
But then again it might."

"That's exactly right," said Miss Lynne.

This time all the kids laughed. And so did Miss Lynne. She realized she had added to Yoko's rhyme.

Maya took a closer look at the prow of the ship. "That creature looks like an eagle from the front, but it has legs and a tail like a lion."

Julian and Mac leaned in.

"It looks like a video game character," said Mac.

"Or a character in a fairy tale or a myth," said Julian.

"The ship was named the Griffon. Do you think that has anything to do with this creature?" asked Yoko.

Julian clicked and then read from his tablet. "The griffon is found in Greek and Egyptian legends. It has the body, tail, and back legs of a lion. Its upper body has the head, wings, and talons of an eagle. The griffon guards treasures."

Mac turned to Maya. "Your street is named after a legendary creature!"

"I think maybe Maya's street was named after the ship that was named after a legendary creature," suggested Julian.

"The griffon—the creature—guards treasures," Yoko mused. "So it could be that the Griffon—the ship—held treasures."

"Maya's street is not only named after an old ship, it's named after an old treasure ship!" Mac was excited all over again.

"Let's see," said Yoko. She held out her hand and began counting on her fingers. "We went to the park to hunt for a dogwood and we found what might be a cannonball."

"We came to the library to see what we could learn about the maybe-cannonball, and we found a model of the Griffon," Julian added.

"Now I want to know more about the Griffon," said Lacey.

"And if the cannonball came from the Griffon." Yoko glanced at Julian. "The maybe-cannonball," she corrected herself before he had a chance.

"How do we figure out if the Griffon and the maybe-cannonball are connected?" asked Maya.

Lacey opened her notebook again.

CHAPTER THIRTEEN

Narrow
the Search

Mac looked around the room. "There are so many artifacts here! My head is getting fuzzy!"

Yoko looked at Mac's coonskin cap and giggled.

Julian recalled what Mrs. Schieber had said. "Let's start with what we know. Then we can figure out what we need to find out."

Mac groaned.

"What do we do when we want to find out something, like who invented Pac Man, or when the next superhero action figure in the series is coming out?" asked Julian.

"We look it up on the internet," said Mac.

"We type in a question."

Maya nodded. "We have to come up with a question before we look for an answer."

Miss Lynne patted her shoulder. "That's called narrowing the search. And once you do that, research becomes easier to tackle."

Yoko liked the sound of that.

"Narrow the search, zero in

Then you're ready to begin.

Focus on a question or two

Look for answers, find a clue."

Lacey's pencil was ready. "What do we want to know?"

"I'm curious about the Griffon," said Maya. "Who built it and why? What was it used for?"

"Could the maybe-cannonball have been fired from the Griffon?" asked Yoko.

"Did the Griffon have a cannon?" Julian wondered.

"Did it fire the cannon? Mac added.

Lacey read their questions back to them. "Let's keep these questions in mind as we investigate."

Miss Lynne looked at her watch. "The library closes in an hour." She sat down and pulled a stack of students' papers and a green pen with a T. rex on top from her bag. "I'm going to grade these papers. Let me know if I can help with anything."

The kids circled the room.

They read.

They wondered.

They thought.

And they learned.

Lacey moved back and forth between her friends. She took pages of notes.

It was exciting. It was fun!

But after awhile, Lacey's hand was tired from writing.

Julian's shirt was untucked and rumpled.

Maya yawned.

Yoko rested her head in her hand.

Mac flipped the tail on his hat from one side of his head to the other. He did it again. And again.

Lacey was rubbing her fingers when the librarian stepped in. "The library will be closing in ten minutes."

Miss Lynne stretched and stuffed the papers and pen into her bag. "Research—and correcting papers—is hard work," she said. "You know what I think?" She kept her voice low. "It's time for cookies and lemonade!"

The friends clapped…softly. They were in the library, after all.

CHAPTER FOURTEEN

Is It Important?

The kids settled on Miss Lynne's porch with a tray of lemonade and cookies. Pesky wagged his tail. He seemed happy to be with his friends. And happy when a crumb or two fell to the floor.

Lacey tucked her feet beneath her and laid her notebook on her lap.

"Our list of facts is long," she said.

"Read us one at a time. If it doesn't answer our questions, we can cross it out," suggested Maya.

"Agreed," Julian said. "If it doesn't tell us something about the Griffon and the cannon, it's not important to our research."

Lacey began reading.

• Father Hennepin erected a church on Cayuga Island around 1678-1679.

"I live on Hennepin Avenue," said Mac. "Now I know where the name came from."

"That is awesome," said Julian. "But it doesn't answer our questions."

The kids agreed. Lacey crossed it out and read the next fact.

• Father Hennepin was a priest who came with the explorer Rene-Robert Cavelier, Sieur de LaSalle to the New World.

"Wow, that's a long name!" said Mac. "I wouldn't want to be that explorer learning how to spell my name in kindergarten."

Yoko giggled. "True," she agreed. "But that fact doesn't help us."

Lacey drew a line through the fact.

Mac swayed back and forth on the porch swing. He liked that it hung from ropes hooked into the ceiling.

• The Griffon was a ship built by LaSalle, Father Hennepin, and others.

"Well…"said Maya, "that's a fact about the Griffon." She pulled a lone droopy dandelion from her shoe. "But it doesn't tell us anything about the cannon."

• The Griffon launched in July 1679.

"That could be important," said Julian.

"Why?" Yoko wiped a splash of lemonade on her sunglasses with a corner of her shirt.

"Because if we figure out how old the cannonball is, we'll know if it could be from the

Griffon," said Julian.

Yoko high-fived Julian.

- The Griffon may have been the first sailing vessel built by explorers to sail the upper Great Lakes.

"Wow! And it was built right here." Maya paused. "But I guess that's not important for our research."

The friends agreed.

Zip. Lacey crossed it out.

- The Griffon may have been larger than any other vessel on the lakes at the time.

"Same," said Julian.

- The Griffon is known to have been a 40 ton vessel with three masts, a foremast, main and mizzen, and several square sails.

"Cool beans!" said Mac. He looked at his friends. "But not important?"

Heads nodded, and Lacey crossed it out.

- The Griffon was armed with seven cannons.

"Important!" all the kids shouted at once.

Lacey put a star next to that fact.

- The Griffon launched in the Cayuga Creek channel of the upper Niagara River with the roar of her cannons.

  "Very important!" said Julian.

  Lacey put two stars next to that fact.

- The Griffon was armed with two cannons and three rail guns.

  "Very, very important!" said Mac.

  "Wait a minute," said Lacey. "This says two cannons." She ran her finger up the page, "but here it says 'seven cannons'."

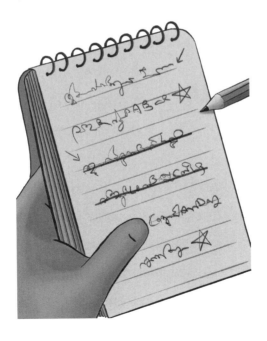

Maya's brows bunched. "That doesn't make sense."

"Finding facts that don't match can happen when doing research," said Miss Lynne. "You'll have to recheck your sources. Make sure you got it right."

Stink bug! Mac thought to himself.

"That's why when we were at the library you suggested we write down the sources of the facts we collected," said Yoko.

"But what if we did get it right?" asked Maya. "What if sources have different information?"

"Then you can try to determine which source is more credible or believable," said Miss Lynne.

Mac groaned. "That means even more research."

Lacey circled the facts that didn't agree. "Think of it this way. Doing research is like being a detective. Some leads—or facts—are helpful..."

"And some are just confusing," said Maya.

Lacey read the next fact:

- La Salle, seeking the Northwest Passage to China and Japan, sailed the Griffon across Lake Erie, Lake Huron, and Lake Michigan.

"China and Japan!" exclaimed Yoko. "You can't get there from the Great Lakes!"

Julian laughed. "Well, we know that now, but back then the explorers were, well, exploring. They didn't know that yet."

Lacey kept reading. The next two facts didn't answer any of their questions. But the fact after that did.

- ~~The Griffon sailed to the interior of North America, where previously only canoes had traveled.~~
- ~~The Griffon was filled with furs~~
- The Griffon landed in Michigan to trade goods for furs with Native Americans

Lacey read the final three facts:

- La Salle got off the ship and sent it back to Niagara.
- The Griffon disappeared along the way.
- The Griffon never returned to Niagara and has never been found.

Suddenly, Mac was excited again. "This is turning out to be just like a real mystery!"

"The Griffon and that cannonball aren't *like* real mysteries, they *are* real mysteries," said Lacey, closing her notebook.

The Cayuga Island Kids had learned so much.

They knew who built the Griffon. And they knew why.

But was the maybe-cannonball a *for-sure* cannonball? Was it fired from the Griffon?

The kids had some answers. They just didn't have *all* the answers. There was more to find out. But that was okay. Tomorrow was another day of summer vacation.

Chapter Fifteen

Day Two

L acey awoke to a tickle. A ticklish spray. She opened her eyes. Cold drops of water were coming through the open window.

It was raining. Hard. Lacey sat up quickly. She wiped her face with the sheet and put her feet on the floor.

Now they were wet, too. Lacey looked down to find a thin puddle. Her toes were right smack in the middle of it.

She was about to close the window when Pesky bounded into her room. He rounded the side of the bed. He hit the puddle. *Splash!* Now Lacey was wet up to her knees.

Pesky jumped up and wagged his drippy tail.

"Ack!" Lacey sputtered. She felt wet from head to toe. And it wasn't a fun wet like splashing in the pool at Auntie RoRo's house or playing in the sprinkler slide on Yoko's lawn.

But Pesky didn't seem to mind being wet. He yipped and wagged and wagged and yipped.

Lacey laughed and patted her pup. "Let's go find a towel," she said. On the way, she closed the window.

Mac looked out the window above the kitchen sink. It was dark even though it was morning. Rain splashed from the gutters. Wavy ribbons of water dribbled down the panes of glass. Everything in the yard looked crooked.

Mac turned on the faucet to fill his glass. Outside the window, he noticed a chipmunk scurrying across the patio. It dodged planters and weaved between railings. Mac leaned forward as the chipmunk disappeared under the chair cover.

Water from the faucet sprayed Mac's pajama top. It trickled to his toes. Mac shook off the water and wiped his hands on his pajama pants. He'd clean up the dribbles on the floor later. Right now, he was hungry.

Just as he reached into the cupboard for the box of Pop-Pops, thunder cracked. Mac jumped and cereal scattered. It landed on the counter. It landed on the wet floor. It even landed in Mac's hair.

"Stink bug!" said Mac. He stepped around the cereal and reached for his frontiersman bowl. He slid his arm across the counter, clearing spilled cereal to make space for the jug of milk. He'd clean the counter later. Right now, he was hungry.

Julian was eating his breakfast and reading the back of the cereal box when the phone buzzed.

"Hi," said Mac. "What are you doing?" Julian could hear Mac chewing on the other end of the phone.

"The same thing you're doing," said Julian. "I'm eating breakfast. And I'm reading."

"How do you know I'm eating breakfast?" Mac asked around a mouth full of cereal.

Julian laughed. "It's no mystery. The clue is I can hear you munching."

"Sorry," said Mac before chomping on another spoonful.

"Did you know that puffed cereals are made using a pressure-cooking method? It's called "gun-puffing." Quaker Oats used a cannon converted into a pressure cooker in the early 1900s."

Mac stopped chewing and studied his spoonful of Pop-Pops. "No way!" He jumped off his stool and opened the lower cupboard. "My mom has one of those!"

"A cannon?" Julian joked. He laughed when he heard Mac laughing. He pictured milk spraying out of his friend's nose.

"If you can make a pressure cooker out of a cannon, I wonder if I could make a cannon out of Mom's pressure cooker," said Mac. "Speaking of cannons," he interrupted himself, "how are we going to work on solving our mystery today?"

Julian looked out the window. The sky was jammed with dark clouds. The sun was nowhere in sight. "Rainy days are perfect for reading research," he said.

Mac didn't answer. But Julian could hear him chewing.

Maya was chewing on the end of her hair ribbon. She was searching the closet for her most favorite purple umbrella. It was the perfect day to use it—as soon as she knew where she was going, of course.

The umbrella was propped beside Maya's most favorite purple rubber boots. Now she was really eager to know where she was going today. She had two favorites to wear—not counting the purple satin ribbon she would tie in her hair.

Thunder cracked. The sound brought to mind the cannonball they had discovered yesterday. Tingles tickled Maya's spine every time she thought of it.

Sparky's tail fluffed out as she skittered across the room and into Maya's closet. The cat huddled in the middle of a pile of mostly purple dancing scarves. Sparky did not like thunder.

Maya drew her cat onto her lap. "You definitely would not like being a passenger on the Griffon," she murmured. She nuzzled Sparky and rubbed her ears. "It wouldn't matter if it had seven cannons or two!"

Suddenly, like a bolt of lightning, a thought came to Maya. "That's it!" She jumped up and twirled, hugging her cat to her chest. "Thank you, Sparky! Wait until I tell the others!"

Sparky squinted at Maya and purred.

Maya gently put her cat back on the pile of scarves in the closet. Now she knew where she was going. She had to meet up with her friends!

Meanwhile, Yoko was dreaming of explorers and griffons. She was sailing the Great Lakes. It was cold and windy. The water was choppy.

A loud noise woke her, and she opened her eyes. Were those cannons firing in the distance? She looked left and right. Was that a pile of furs?

No, she was not sailing on the Griffon. She was in her bedroom. And those weren't furs. It was just her fuzzy buffalo blanket bunched into a heap.

Boom!

And those weren't cannons firing. It was thunder!

Yoko looked out the window. The wind was blowing. It was cold and rainy.

"Thunder claps, lightning zaps

spark and boom through my room."

Yoko stretched and pulled her blanket to her chin.

A summer storm always made her want to snuggle under the covers.

Yoko closed her eyes.

Could she get back to her dream? She thought about the explorers. She thought about the Griffon. She thought about the maybe-cannonball.

Suddenly she had an idea.

Yoko threw back the covers. She had to tell her friends.

Chapter Sixteen

Rainy Day, Bright Ideas

Yoko stood on Julian's porch. She jiggled with excitement as she peeked from under her sopping hood.

"Come on in," said Julian. "Mac's here and Lacey is on her way."

"Maya is coming, too," Mac called from the kitchen. "She just needs to find her most favorite purple something or other and then she'll be right over."

Yoko hung her very wet hoodie on a hook. "It's probably her purple slicker," she said. "It's really raining hard." Whatever it was, Yoko hoped Maya found it right away. She was eager to share her idea, but she would wait until everyone arrived.

Julian led the way into the kitchen and was just about to offer Yoko some juice when the doorbell rang again.

"It's open!" Mac called out.

Lacey kicked off her soggy sneakers and shook out her hair. She hadn't brought an umbrella or worn a jacket. Why bother? She had started the day off wet from head to toe. Her notebook was dry, though. Lacey had tucked it safely beneath her shirt in the waistband of her jeans.

Now, Lacey pulled it out. She flipped to the last page of notes. "Yesterday was an exciting day. Mysteries. Hunts. Discoveries. Lots of questions. And some answers."

"Which led to more questions," said Mac.

Yoko looked out the window. "Too bad it's raining today."

"It's a great day for reading research," said Mac.

Julian laughed. Mac had been listening to him on the phone after all.

Julian placed a stack of glasses on the table beside the juice. "Help yourself," he said. The doorbell rang again, and Julian let Maya in.

"I figured something out!" Maya sprang onto her toes. She couldn't wait to tell her friends. "It doesn't matter if the Griffon had two cannons or seven cannons, or whatever number of cannons. As long as it had one, the cannonball we found—if it is a cannonball—could have been fired from the ship!"

Lacey tilted her head to one side. "Right!" She flipped through her notebook and landed on the page of facts. "According to all the sources we checked, there was at least one cannon on the Griffon."

Yoko felt like corn was popping in her belly. She couldn't wait any longer to share her idea with her friends. "I had a dream last night that gave me an idea," she announced.

"Dreams are good like that," said Julian.

"I didn't get any ideas about how to find a dogwood," said Mac, "or how to make arrows from dogwoods. And I was thinking about that all night long." Mac refilled his glass of juice.

"Anyway," Julian said, "what's your idea, Yoko?" He would keep his friends on track.

"You reminded us to start with what we know," said Yoko, "like Mrs. Schieber told us." She took a deep breath. "We know the Griffon was built right here on our island. We discovered a maybe-cannonball in the park. We learned that the explorers built the Griffon there." She paused to take another breath. "And," she nodded toward Maya, "we know the ship had at least one cannon. What we don't know is if the maybe-cannonball is actually a cannonball, and if it is from the Griffon."

"That's two mysteries," Lacey said.

"We need an expert," said Yoko.

"Mrs. Schieber?" asked Mac.

"I think we need to find someone who can look at the maybe-cannonball and tell us if it is a for-sure cannonball," said Yoko.

"And if it is," said Julian slowly, "could it have been shot from the Griffon."

"How do we find that expert?" asked Mac.

"Research!" said Julian.

"I knew you'd say that," said Mac.

Julian turned on his tablet.

Lacey flipped to a new page in her notebook.

Outside, it was still raining. But that didn't matter.

Inside, the Cayuga Island Kids were busy doing research.

CHAPTER SEVENTEEN

Teamwork

When the doorbell rang again, Mac looked around the room.

"Who could that be?" he asked. His friends were all here. Well, except for Pesky. Even though he was a very smart dog and could probably figure out how to ring the doorbell, Mac didn't think he could reach it.

"Another mystery," said Lacey.

Maya rose on her toes and looked out the window.

"It's Mr. Esposito," she said. "He's carrying a lumpy sack over his shoulder."

Julian pushed back his chair and rose to

answer the door.

Yoko stood beside Maya at the window. She could see Mr. Esposito had a cap on. Rain dripped from the visor. It dripped from his coat. He was making a puddle on Julian's porch. Just like that, a rhyme popped into Yoko's head.

"The wind is whipping, Mr. E. is dripping,

And the sack he's gripping is slipping!"

Mac raced past Julian to get to the door. "Mr. Esposito is not a drip! He's very nice."

"I didn't say…" Yoko said.

Mac flung open the door.

"You're dripping!" said Mac.

"I am," agreed Mr. Esposito. "And this sack is slipping. May I come in?"

Julian hung his neighbor's coat on the last hook.

Mr. Esposito carefully lowered the heavy sack. "Since it's raining outside, I can't work in the park," he said. "So I can help with your research instead."

Mr. Esposito opened the sack and removed a smaller bag. Inside that was the maybe-cannonball wrapped in paper towels.

"We found some photos of cannonballs that seem to match this one." Julian showed Mr. Esposito a series of photos.

"We were narrowing the search," said Lacey.

"Smart," said Mr. Esposito.

"Some are too big," said Julian.

"Some are too small," said Maya.

"Some don't look like they are made of the same metal," said Yoko.

"It's sort of like Goldilocks and the porridge," said Mac.

"We are also trying to find out what size cannonball the Griffon may have used," said Maya.

"We need an expert to help us figure out if the maybe-cannonball is actually a cannonball, and if it could be from the Griffon," said Lacey.

"I may be able to help with that." Mr. Esposito pulled a wad of damp, folded papers out of his pocket.

He unfolded the papers and smoothed them out. "Dr. Sylvia Spina, one of my golf partners—when I used to play golf—is an archaeologist."

"A what?" said Mac.

"An archaeologist," Mr. Esposito repeated.

"Archaeology is the study of artifacts usually dug up from the ground." Julian looked at his friends. He could tell they wondered how he knew that. "Archaeology was one of the words on my calendar."

"Ah." Lacey nodded.

"Do you think she will help us?" Yoko asked Mr. Esposito.

He unfolded the papers. "I have Sylvia's home, office, and cell phone numbers right here. Let's find out."

CHAPTER EIGHTEEN

Questions

The next day the sun was shining again. Mr. Esposito wore his cap, but it was no longer dripping. He waved to Maya as he set off for the park.

Maya waved back. After all that rain, Mr. Esposito would have plenty to do in the park. He would be busy—and muddy—today.

But yesterday he was able to reach Dr. Sylvia Spina, archaeologist. They talked on the phone. He laughed and nodded his head. He winked at the kids, who were all watching and waiting. When Mr. Esposito finally finished nodding and talking, he gave them the good news. His friend was eager to see the maybe-cannonball.

"Sylvia doesn't get wound up about many things. But," Mr. Esposito's eyes crinkled, "when she heard about what you found in the park, she said, 'Intriguing!' For Sylvia, that's as good as jumping up and down and clapping at the same time."

Mac tried jumping up and down and clapping at the same time. It was fun.

Dr. Spina had agreed to meet the kids and Mr. Esposito at the park garage at four o'clock.

Maya was excited. Thanks to Mr. Esposito, they had found an artifact expert—an archaeologist! Dr. Spina was kind to offer to help.

Maya decided right then to make Dr. Spina a thank you card. She would use real flower petals and curly ribbon. She would write THANK

YOU in fancy letters with her favorite purple glitter pen. All her friends could sign it.

Just thinking about it made Maya smile. She twirled toward the backyard garden. After she picked the flowers, she planned to check the spelling of *archaeologist*. Her head was full of thank you thoughts.

Yoko's head was full of thoughts, too. Getting to meet an archaeologist was exciting.

And Sylvia Spina was a very flowy name.

Yoko imagined Sylvia Spina with long wavy hair flowing to her waist.

She imagined Sylvia Spina as tall and strong.

She probably wore steel-toed boots to the dig sites. And safety goggles.

Yoko pictured Sylvia Spina gliding in a flowy way, even though she wore steel-toed boots.

Yoko imagined Sylvia Spina as having a flowy, rippling laugh. And she imagined hearing that laugh when she shared a rhyme about her.

Yoko wondered what words rhymed with Sylvia Spina. Well, she had the whole day to work on that.

Yoko could hardly wait to meet Sylvia Spina.

Julian could hardly wait to meet Dr. Spina, either. A real live archaeologist!

He wondered if she dug up artifacts all day. Where would she do that?

Or did she spend most of her time studying artifacts that were already dug up?

Where would the artifacts come from? Were they delivered to her? How did she study them? What clues did she look for? How did she know what clues to look for?

What would Dr. Spina think of the maybe-cannonball?

Julian had so many questions. And the more questions he thought of, the more excited he was to meet Dr. Spina.

Mac was excited, too.

And worried.

Would Dr. Spina want to take the maybe-cannonball somewhere to study it?

What if that took a long time? What if they never saw it again?

Mac wondered if Dr. Spina had ever dug up a dinosaur bone. How would she know it was a dinosaur bone and not a steak bone some lucky dog had buried?

Mac wondered if dust and dirt from all that digging makes an archaeologist sneeze.

Did Dr. Spina keep a giant box of tissues at her desk? Did she have a desk?

Did she have a collection of fossils?

Had Dr. Spina ever seen hieroglyphics? Could she tell what the symbols meant?

Mac's head was spinning.

Lacey's head was spinning, too.

She thought about all the history that had taken place right here on Cayuga Island—and she hadn't even known about it until three days ago!

She thought about the explorers of the Niagara Frontier.

She thought about the Griffon.

And she thought about the maybe-cannonball, of course.

Lacey flipped open her notebook and read over her notes again. This sure was one exciting mystery.

She carefully unfolded the tissue holding the bit of metal that had fallen from the ball. She looked at it closely. It beat anything she had found—or hoped to find—in any of the alleys on Cayuga Island.

Did it hold any clues? It just looked like a metal flake to her. But maybe it could help Dr. Spina crack this case. Lacey folded up the tissue and tucked it in her pocket. Her heart raced with excitement.

Meanwhile, Pesky raced in his dream.

Lacey had stayed up way too late last night flipping the pages of big thick library books. So Pesky had stayed awake, too.

After all, a dog never knows when his person might get hungry from all that page flipping and decide to go hunting for a late-night snack.

And it's a dog's job to follow his person wherever they go. Especially when they go hunting. And most especially when they go hunting for a late-night snack.

Morning inched its way to afternoon. Finally, it was time for the kids to head to the park.

Maya slipped into her most favorite purple flip flops. She tucked the thank you card she had made into her most favorite purple plastic purse that looked just like the one in her most favorite picture book about a plastic purse.

Yoko put on her sunglasses and skipped out the door. In her mind she went over the words she had thought of that rhymed with Sylvia Spina. *Spiralina, concertina, Wilhemina.* None of them made much sense in a poem about an archaeologist. She would keep thinking on her way to the park.

Mac was ready when Julian came by. He had a question for his best friend. But before Mac had a chance to ask it, Lacey and Pesky hurried up the sidewalk. Maya and Yoko were waiting at the corner.

Together, the friends walked toward the park.

Mac was jumpy. Julian could tell by the way he sort of hop-walked.

"Everything okay?" Julian asked.

Mac nodded yes. Then he shook his head no. "Do you think Sylvia Spina will take away our cannonball?" he blurted.

"I hope so," Julian said. When Mac frowned, Julian explained. "That would mean she wants to study it."

"What if we never see it again?" Mac worried.

Julian put his arm around his friend's shoulders. "We might see it in a science magazine, or on the news, or even in a museum."

Lacey paused while Pesky sniffed a tree. "I wonder if Dr. Spina will let us visit her lab—or," her eyes brightened, "a dig site! I'd love to see an archaeologist at work."

"Me, too," Julian said.

Maya pointed. Up ahead, Mr. Esposito stood outside the park garage. Beside him a short, round woman with spiky red hair was laughing. "It looks like we'll find out soon."

CHAPTER NINETEEN

An Afternoon of Answers

Inside the park garage, Mr. Esposito had laid a clean white plastic sheet across the potting table. The maybe-cannonball rested there. A bright light dangled from the rafters above it. Dr. Spina and the kids gathered around.

Dr. Spina was silent as she bent over the round metal ball. She examined it carefully. "Hmmm," she murmured.

Dr. Spina moved her head from side to side. She studied the ball from all angles as if it were a rare jewel.

"Hmmm," she murmured again.

Dr. Spina pulled a shiny metal tool about the size of a pencil from her shirt pocket. She used it to turn the maybe-cannonball slowly. Fine bits of metal fell onto the plastic sheet. Sylvia Spina swept the dust into a pile with a tiny brush she had pulled from the same shirt pocket. She rubbed the dust gently between her fingers. She held it to her nose. She sniffed.

Lacey took the tissue holding the metal flake from the park out of her pocket. She offered it to Dr. Spina "This came off the ball when we were digging it up, and I saved it. I thought it might be a clue."

"Ah!" Dr. Spina gently lifted the thin metal piece from the tissue. She turned it over and studied it some more.

Her sturdy boot tap-tap-tapped on the cement floor.

The kids watched as Dr. Spina leaned in close. She looked at the metal flake. She looked at the ball. Then she looked at the flake again.

They kept silent when she said "hmmm" again.

Mac was counting. Dr. Spina had said "hmmm" three times. He wondered what "hmmm" meant when an archaeologist said it three times. It was hard to wait. He was eager to know.

Mac looked at his friends. He could tell they were eager to know, too.

Julian was holding his breath.

A row of squiggles crossed Lacey's forehead. It looked like his paper when he tried to draw straight lines without a ruler.

Maya was standing still. Neither of her feet was moving.

Even Yoko was paying attention instead of daydreaming. Her eyes were fixed on Dr. Spina.

Finally, Dr. Spina straightened. "May I?" she asked, holding her hands just above the ball.

"Sure," said Mr. Esposito.

Dr. Spina carefully lifted the maybe-cannonball. She held it an arm's length away. Slowly she lowered it a few inches. She lifted and lowered it again.

"Hmmm," she said.

Mac fidgeted.

Maya adjusted her purse.

Yoko's eyes drifted to the ceiling.

Julian cleared his throat.

Lacey fingered her notebook in her back pocket.

Mr. Esposito rocked back and forth. He removed his cap and ran his hands through his hair. "What do you think, Sylvia?" he spouted. He replaced his cap and tugged it into place. "The suspense is killing me!"

The kids seemed to take in one long breath and let it out.

Dr. Spina smiled and placed the ball back on the table. She fingered the new sprinkle of metal dust it had made.

"Hmmm," she said once more.

She crossed her arms. She drummed her fingers on her elbows. Then she turned and faced the kids. "Here's what I know for sure," she began.

Lacey pulled the notebook from her pocket. She slid the pencil from behind her ear.

"This is indeed a cannonball…" Dr. Spina began.

She paused while the kids and Mr. Esposito cheered.

"It is old. And it's made of iron," she continued. "I was sure once I saw that metal flake." She smiled at Lacey. "And my guess is that the cannonball weighs about ten or twelve pounds." Dr. Spina shrugged her shoulders. "Figuring all that out was easy."

Lacey stopped writing and looked up.

"What we don't know—what we can't know—is whether this cannonball came from the Griffon," Dr. Spina said quietly. "The ship sank somewhere in the Great Lakes in 1679. Since it was never found, there is no way to know if this cannonball is from the ship."

Lacey stopped writing. "A cold case," she said.

"A what?" Mac said.

"A cold case," Lacey repeated. "The mystery of the Griffon was never solved. But it took place so long ago, it isn't being investigated anymore."

Julian sagged.

Maya slumped.

Yoko thoughts swirled. *Oh no! I hate to think we'll never know.*

"But, like any cold case," added Dr. Spina, "it remains open. If new information about the Griffon were to be discovered, it would spur investigation."

Julian nodded. The disappointment he felt was reflected in his friends' faces. "However," Dr. Spina clapped her hands together. Her eyes sparkled. "The fact remains that you," she spread her arms wide to include all of the kids, "have uncovered an artifact!"

"Like all that stuff in the library!" Mac thought about jumping up and down and clapping his hands. Instead, he fist-bumped Julian.

Dr. Spina smiled at the brightened faces around her. "This cannonball has a story. It is a piece of Cayuga Island history—whether it's from the Griffon or from another chapter in the island's past. I'm looking forward to examining it more closely to learn what clues it has for us."

"So…" Maya's eyes widened, "we *maybe* discovered a piece of the Griffon's story."

Julian let out a puff of air. "This *for-sure* cannonball may be part of one of the biggest unsolved mysteries ever to take place in the Great Lakes!"

"And," Lacey hugged her notebook to her chest, "in the history of Cayuga Island."

Yoko giggled. "I like that. The biggest mystery in our island's history!"

"Hmmm." Dr. Spina looked at each of the kids and nodded. "I would tend to agree."

CHAPTER TWENTY

Mystery Solved

The friends walked across the park toward home. Wind was blowing through the trees and clouds were forming. It felt like it might rain again. But the kids weren't paying attention to the clues that another summer storm was on its way.

"I'm glad Dr. Spina agreed to take the cannonball to study it some more," Mac said.

"Hmmm." Julian's head swiveled and he grinned at his friend.

"I hope someday we learn more about the Griffon mystery. Maybe the cannonball will be a clue that helps, or maybe it will unlock some other mystery," Lacey said.

"Dr. Spina is sure to learn something from our artifact," said Julian.

Lacey smiled widely. "Just knowing that the cannonball we discovered is an artifact is pretty exciting."

"And your wish is coming true," said Maya.

Lacey looked at her, confused.

"You said you wished you could visit an archaeological dig site, and we can!" Maya explained. "We can go to the park and watch Dr. Spina dig up the area where we found the cannonball."

Mac nodded. "I bet she finds more of those metal flakes like the one you gave her."

"Even Mr. Esposito is excited that she's going to be digging in the park!" Maya kidded.

"Besides the dig, I can't wait to visit her lab," said Julian.

"That is going to be fab," Yoko agreed.

"It was really nice of her to invite us," said Julian.

Maya held her hands to her heart. "I'm so happy Dr. Spina liked the card we gave her."

The kids paused while Pesky sniffed a lamp post. He had a mystery of his own to investigate.

"This case may be cold, but it is not closed." Lacey patted her back pocket where her notebook was safely stowed.

Pesky lost interest in his mystery, and the kids continued walking. They spotted Miss Lynne covering her porch swing. She was stacking a pile of papers and a cup and saucer. She waved to the kids. "Another storm is brewing!" She pointed to the sky. "Time to batten down the hatches!"

Mac wasn't sure what *batten down the hatches* meant, but he figured it had something to do with getting ready for a storm.

Yoko and Maya headed toward Griffon Avenue.

"See you tomorrow!" Maya said to the others. The wind gusted and her hair curled around her face like a pair of fluffy earphones.

"See you later, alligator!" Yoko linked arms with Maya and they skipped off.

Julian, Mac, and Lacey walked a little faster. At Lacey's house, Mac leaned over to rub Pesky's ear. Lacey promised to show Julian the library books she had checked out before she returned them.

On Hennepin Avenue, Julian and Mac spotted Mrs. Schieber. She was gathering garden tools into her wheelbarrow.

"More rain is on the way!" she called out. She pointed to the trees. "Look at the way the leaves are turning in on themselves. Better get home."

Mac held onto his coonskin cap. The tail tickled his ear as it swung in the wind. Julian hugged his tablet to his chest.

When they reached his house, Mac checked the mailbox and fist-bumped his friend. Julian had a block to go to reach home.

Mac turned up the driveway and stopped. He thought he heard a dog barking. Had Pesky gotten loose? He looked around, but there was no dog in sight. He shrugged and continued along the sidewalk to the door. A raindrop hit his cheek. Then another and another. The wind swirled. A leaf fluttered down and landed on his powder horn. Another landed on his nose. Mac looked up. And then he eyes grew wide.

The branches of the tree next to his house were rubbing together. And they sounded just like a dog barking.

Mac bounded up the porch steps. "Mom!" he yelled. "Is that a dogwood tree in our front yard?"

Turn the page to see the real cannonball and take a sneak peek at the next book in the

Cayuga Island Kids

series!

Is This Story Fact or Fiction?

The Mystery of the Barking Branches and the Sunken Ship is both **fact** and **fiction**, because it is based on a true story (fact) but the characters and their adventures are made up (fiction).

The **setting**, or where the story takes place, is real. I grew up on Cayuga Island. It is located exactly where it says it is in the story—a few miles upstream from the mighty Niagara Falls. I've modified the island a bit to fit the story, but overall, if you were to visit you'd find it to be pretty much the way it is described. Changing a few details of a real place is something an author might do in order to better serve a made-up or **fictional** story.

The **characters** in the Cayuga Island Kids series are **fictional**. They are not real children or adults; however, some of their **characteristics** are based on real people. Parts of their personalities, or what they do, eat, say, or think, are based on the actions of people I know. Real people (and pets!) often inspire fictional characters.

The **plot**, or the events that take place in the story, are **fictional**. What happens in the story came straight from my imagination. However, some important elements in the story are **factual.**

- The cannonball is real! It was found buried in Mike Esposito's backyard when a fence was being installed. Mike Esposito's backyard is across the street from the park on Cayuga Island. Here is a photograph of the actual cannonball.

Does Mike Esposito's name sound familiar? He is the real person upon whom the fictional character, Mr. Esposito, is based. The real Mr. Esposito is a history teacher at Niagara Falls High School in Niagara Falls, New York. He has a warmhearted wife and five terrific kids who enjoy a variety of organized sports as well as just playing around in the park on Cayuga Island.

- The Griffon was really a ship. It was built on Cayuga Island in 1679 for the purpose of fur-trading. On an early voyage, the ship sank and has never been found. It remains one of the greatest mysteries of the Great Lakes.

Want to learn more about the Griffon, explorers of the Niagara Frontier, the Great Lakes, Niagara Falls, or the rich history of Cayuga Island? How about dogwood trees? I learned about barking branches during my research on dogwood trees—and that interesting piece of information ended up in the story and in the title!

Investigate topics of interest in your school or public library and on safe online sites, just as the Cayuga Island Kids do. Remember what Mrs. Schieber recommends: Always check more than one source. Be a fact detective. Make sure the information is accurate—that it's **fact**, not **fiction.**

Find Cayuga Island Kids activities and an educator's guide at **www.judybradbury.com** *and on* **CityofLightPublishing.com**.

Coming in Fall 2021!
Book Two
of the

Cayuga Island
Kids

series

The Adventure of the Big Fish by the Small Creek

Story by Judy Bradbury

Illustrations by Gabriella Vagnoli

I t was the middle of summer vacation, and Lacey was eager to solve another mystery. The Cayuga Island Kids had puzzled over two mysteries so far this summer—and they had solved one of them. Lacey had marked the hunt for barking branches CASE CLOSED in her notebook.

The other mystery would take plenty of experts plenty more time to solve—probably even longer than the summer. After all, no one had cracked the case of the sunken ship, the Griffon—built right here on Cayuga Island—in over 300 years!

But that's history. That was the beginning of summer vacation.

This morning the friends would meet in the park. No mystery there. They met in the park most days in the summer. But where could they search for a mystery?

Lacey and Pesky cut through the alley on the way to the park. It would take longer, but it was more mysterious. And that meant it was more fun. Lacey would hunt for clues on the way to meet her friends.

Pesky hunted, too. He sniffed, his nose close to the ground. He darted from one side of the dusty gravel path to the other.

"Yip!" Pesky yapped. Two dented garbage cans! A heap of musty leaves! An old tire!

"Yip! Yip!" They all smelled terrific!

While Pesky sniffed, Lacey observed.

There stood the wooden trellis beside Mrs. Schieber's garden shed. Lacey knew she had been working in her garden. A wet trowel was drying in the sun near the rolled up hose.

Timmy Winslow's rusty green tricycle rested beneath a trio of tired bushes. Lacey knew that Timmy hadn't ridden it for a while because a maze of cobwebs laced the wheels.

One squirrel chased another around a bale of wire leaning against the trunk of a maple tree. A knotted string of tiny lights lay across a woodpile. Were Timmy and his dad planning another project? Were they about to add to Timmy's treehouse?

Lacey sighed. She had seen all of this before.

As she continued down the alley, Lacey spotted something shiny. She paused to investigate. With the toe of her sneaker, she pushed aside some gravel. She pulled out her magnifying glass. She leaned over to have a closer look.

The shape reminded her of something. If she turned her head to the side, it almost looked like a fish. Lacey laughed. That, she decided, was just her imagination. What she had discovered wasn't much of anything. It was just a mangled hanger someone had carelessly thrown in the alley. It sure wasn't a clue worth writing in her notebook.

But Lacey knew that a good detective doesn't give up. Even though she tucked her magnifying glass back in her pocket, she kept observing on her way through the alley.

Up ahead in the park, Lacey spotted Julian and Yoko near the edge of the creek. They seemed to be looking at something in the water. Mac and Maya were behind them. Lacey could see Mac's fishing gear, but he wasn't about to catch anything. The pole lay on the ground.

That wasn't the clue that made Lacey hurry along.

Maya stood on her tiptoes peering over Yoko's shoulder. She had her hand over her mouth.

That was a bigger clue.

Something was wrong.

Meet the Author

Judy Bradbury is an author, an award-winning literacy advocate and educator, and host of the popular Children's Book Corner blog. She is also a Cayuga Island Kid. Judy grew up on the island, which is located just a few miles upstream from the mighty Niagara Falls. In the summers, she rode the bicycle her father built for her across the island in search of mysteries to solve. Judy loves visiting schools and libraries to share her books with students, and frequently offers writing workshops.

Meet the Illustrator

Although she has always loved to draw, Gabriella Vagnoli became an illustrator via a circuitous route that allowed her to explore many other interests including theater, music, teaching, and languages. Her work in these fields all had a common thread: communication. And this is what she loves best about illustrating children's books—the opportunity to visually communicate a story in a way that will indelibly imprint it on young minds, just as she still has with her the illustrated stories from her childhood in Italy.